I0611062

GREATER THAN THE
GODS INTENDED

BLAZE WARD

KNOTTED ROAD PRESS

Greater Than The Gods Intended
Blaze Ward
Copyright © 2014 Blaze Ward
All rights reserved
Published by Knotted Road Press
www.KnottedRoadPress.com

ISBN: 978-1-64470-013-6

Cover art: Copyright © Innovari | Dreamstime.com - Spaceship And
Asteroid Field Photo

Cover and interior design copyright © 2015 Knotted Road Press

Never miss a release!
If you'd like to be notified of new releases, sign up for my newsletter.

I will never spam you, or use your email for nefarious purposes. You can
also unsubscribe at any time.

http://www.blazeward.com/newsletter/

PROLOGUE

Marasem soared on the morning thermals, stretching his cobalt-blue wings to their utmost. He turned his head a little and snapped his great, spiked tail at an imaginary foe, practicing for the mating flight he knew was due within months.

So many competitors to breed the Empress.

He would need to be strong, as well as crafty. Only the best dragons succeeded. It was finally his time to show the Great Mother his size and power, to become first among equals.

Below, the rugged landscape unfolded slowly like a piece of cloth pushed together, a land only dragons could master. Wyverns, still retaining the original humanoid form of lizardkind, but with wings added, served well to administer for their masters, but could not soar above these mountains. Even the cursed Malakh, simple elves granted feathered wings by the false god, *Mustafa*, were only pale competition.

Only the dragons were meant to rule.

He banked to his right, a wide circle meant to take in the core of his demesne, lest any invaders think to sneak up on him. Dragons could rule, but they needed armies to conquer. Marasem was alone as far as the tremendous eye could see.

Well enough. The mouth of Marasem's aerie gaped before him.

Below, he could see his soldiers. A team of well-trained troglodyte warriors protected the opening, tracking Marasem across the sky with the ancient siege weapon as he closed. He bellowed a challenge at them, watched the weapon turn and lift to cover the sky again behind him. *Paranoia was only prudence in a truly immortal being.*

Marasem banked into a lazy downward spiral and flattened out a few hundred feet above the sharp rocks. He dropped his tail and back-winged to a near stop, and then settled on the ledge gracefully. He took a moment to inspect his troops, and the afternoon sky, before he sauntered into the first entrance and turned sharply around the tight double-corner hidden just inside.

Someday, one of his enemies would think to rush the entrance and swoop into his cave system before the defenders could respond. He smiled at the sound a dragon would make, flying face-first into solid stone at full speed. He even had a recipe prepared for the feast he would throw, keeping the heart for himself while his warriors gorged on his foe.

ONE

THE ICON

Youngest Brother held the icon with the utmost reverence. He couldn't resist it when his inner eyelid flickered, once, with pure excitement. Closed. Open. The world went slightly fuzzy for a moment through the membrane. His heart fluttered.

He considered the thing he held. None in the village could understand the words it showed nor the sounds it made, cast so long ago in the ancient tongue. The casing tasted of no material recognized, even among the Yoon clan, respected among all lizardkind, throughout the valley, for the delicacy of their tasting senses.

Eldest Brother stood before him and watched as the spasm of religious excitement and doubts rippled down his body, flaring his scales as though a tremendous heat had passed, and twitching the little stub of tail suddenly against the back of his thigh.

Was he truly worthy to undertake this quest?

But doubt was good. Hadn't the Great Mother taught

them that there was always room for doubt, lest one err into arrogance?

And yet…

He could not doubt the surety of this task. For too long, the great lizards, from the Empress Dragon down, had ruled his kind with an iron claw. The troglodytes, at six feet tall, more than twice his own size, practically owned the valley and all the workers and farmers in it. Worse still the Wyverns, for how to make a troglodyte overlord more menacing and arrogant than to give her wings, that she might emulate the Great Mother?

Youngest Brother took a deep breath to settle his nerves. His malachite-colored scales slowly flattened back down. Even the sky grew brighter as his eyes unslitted.

Eldest Brother stared down at him with concern, but also with pride. Two extra inches meant he was the tallest Isaurian in the village, a leader, reinforced by his great cunning. Eldest Brother was very well respected.

He leaned close now to bump snouts with Youngest Brother. "The elders have chosen wisely, Youngest Brother. But always remember that you cannot trust the tall races, nor the scale-less ones. Use them. Abandon them if necessary. Never let them know your true name, lest the evil ones track you here and hurt your family, your village."

Youngest Brother wrapped the icon into a soft leather chamois, and then a rough scrap of cloth. He tucked it into his satchel with care, hidden, and perhaps ignored by a stranger. He smiled a harsh smile, feral. "I would ask the Great Mother to watch over you, Eldest Brother. But that would be wrong, since I seek the tools of vengeance. May you find warm stones and fresh fruit."

Eldest Brother clapped him once on the shoulder as he turned. "Find your luck, Youngest Brother. Find your destiny."

Youngest Brother settled his satchel, his belt, and the straps of his sandals. His shorts were new and well-made leather. They would survive a great journey. He pulled his cape close as he checked the sky. He nodded to himself, and then to Eldest Brother.

He turned and looked at the simple trodden path leading north out of the village. *Thus, the first steps of legend.*

A cry of alarm from the eastern edge of the village ripped the morning sky, followed by bellows of anger and screams of pain.

Both brothers turned towards the sound, and then each other. Youngest Brother was torn by indecision.

Eldest Brother grabbed him by the shoulders and turned him. "The overseers have found us out. You must flee, brother. You must find the tools to free us. Go."

Youngest Brother hesitated yet. The cries came closer. "What of the village?"

Eldest Brother added a soft shove. "If they find the icon, all hope is lost. All the deaths will have been vain."

Youngest Brother took a quick, deep breath. "Then I will become vengeance, Eldest Brother."

He turned and fled into the brush. Behind him, the cries grew terrible.

YOUNGEST BROTHER PEEKED CAREFULLY from underneath a large boulder that was perched on a hill overlooking the great rift valley. In the southern distance, he could just make out a ragged column of Isaurian survivors being quick-marched out of the burning remains of the village by a swarm of troglodyte warriors.

Overhead, tiny at this distance, three wyverns in command glided back and forth. Occasional bursts of magic set more fires. Not just the huts, but now the fields were set alight. Youngest Brother cursed silently.

He watched, still as another rock, until all that remained of his kin disappeared from view, eastward around the curve of a hill. Overhead, only birds moved, predators drawn by the smoke and carnage to feast on the remains of Meng'la. In the west, the sun eased behind the mountains.

Youngest Brother took a deep breath to settle his nerves, stretched close to the breaking point after hours of running and hiding.

He reached into his leather satchel and withdrew the crude map of the southern lands, touching the wrapped icon once for luck. His life had new meaning now, even from this morning. This grand quest, this heroic task, had just been escalated from a liberation to a xenocide.

TWO
THE FREE CITY

Youngest Brother eyed the public house from an alley across the brick-paved street with suspicion as night slowly enveloped the city. Travelers and locals mingled inside and on the stoop out front. Humans, elves, orcs, and even a semi-mythical creature that was an elf from the waist up attached to the body of a monstrous furred quadruped. Truly, the Free City of Varna was a strange and magical place.

Nineteen days of hard travel and hiding had planed Youngest Brother down, physically as well as emotionally. Half a moon of running from rock to rock during the day and napping at night. Time to digest the deaths. Time enough to learn to live with the grief and anger, but not show it.

Youngest Brother had discovered something about himself, perhaps something Eldest Brother and the village leaders had seen. Commitment to the welfare of others and a willingness to work hard were overlaid now with something else. The memory of smoke. Something he would carry always.

He could still rememebr the smell, the screams. Youngest Brother had never been consumed by rage. Before now. He clenched his jaw hard and emerged from the alley with a confident, angry stride, crossing the wide boulevard towards the oasis of light and sound. He reached back and touched a long iron knife tucked into the back of his belt to make sure of where it was. He might need it tonight.

NOTHING in his life could have prepared Youngest Brother for the inside of the tavern. It was too loud. There were magical lights hanging in every corner and over the bar and above the main room, bringing noon inside night without the acrid, choking smoke of burning black shale.

On a raised dais, a mostly naked orc female, twice his height and easily three times his mass, performed some exotic mating dance that involved the feathers of some gigantic bird and occasionally stomping the hands of patrons that got too close or in her way. Unless coins were tossed onto the platform first. That seemed to make it tolerable for her. Youngest Brother shrugged internally. The unscaled were weird.

He sat perched on a short stool along a back wall and clutched a dirty mug of weak fermented juice. Three pucks, half-sized human-like travelers, strangers to himself as well as each other, joined him at a low shelf designed for creatures three feet tall. Obviously, the bar had a wide clientele. He even suspected that, were he to stay long enough, others of his kind would visit. How would he interact with the out-clan?

Such a strange thought. Out-clan. He was out-clan now. Perhaps clanless. Certainly outlaw, if the troglodytes or their wyvern masters found him.

But humans ruled in the Free City. Longer-lived than troglodytes. Faster-breeding than the elves. Rumored, even, to be the First Race, from whom all others were created by the eldest god, **Mustafa**, The Architect of Heaven; and the Great Mother, **Ailaendae**.

Youngest Brother eyed the largely-human crowd and tried to listen for the voice of destiny. In his pouch, the fate of his kind waited to be unlocked. But he needed a specialist to help decipher the meanings. A scholar conversant in the old tongues. A wizard.

Around him, a seething tide of thieves, whores, fences, assassins, and merchants ebbed and flowed. He sipped his fermented juice.

There. Along the near side wall. A group of humans and troglodytes engaged in a superiority contest. Perhaps another mating ritual to establish breeding dominance. The displays were there. One female, unattached. Six males, three men and two lizardmen loosely arrayed around the sixth, a human male, and the female. Angry words. Threatening postures. Dominance games. They were apparently the same across species.

One of the men reared back and threw a fist at the sixth. The target was taller than the others. Darker-skinned. Exotically dressed. He watched the fist clench and begin to flow.

Youngest Brother heard the stars align.

The sixth growled some strange word, audible over the morass of noise, and raised his left hand. A shield of golden energy appeared magically at his wrist and blocked the incoming punch with a grinding crunch. The first screamed in pain and dropped to his knees.

The entire bar went silent.

Youngest Brother dropped his mug in surprise.

He heard the sixth utter a word and point at one of the troglodytes. A mystic bolt emerged from the man's right hand and struck the surprised target dead-center, blasting him backwards several feet. Number three skidded under a table, unconscious or dead.

The wizard turned to number four and blasted him with the same spell while his eldritch shield protected him from the left side.

Youngest Brother watched the sorcerer square angrily on the last three. His shoulders hunched forward. Fingers twitched as he prepared another deadly spell.

The instigator kneeled on the floor and cradled a broken hand close to his chest. Youngest Brother watched the wizard blast him without pity and then point at the last human and last lizardman standing. He growled. Both raised their hands in submissive posture and backed carefully away.

Youngest Brother forgot his lost drink and remembered to breathe. His inner eyelid nictated once in excitement. Blurry. Clear. Inside, he smiled.

Across the room, the wizard returned to his booth with unchallenged dominance of his mating claim. Youngest Brother watched the woman and tried to evaluate her as breeding stock. Human, so twice his size. Curved of hip and chest in a way that troglodytes or his own kind only rarely achieved. And hair. A strangely-braided reddish rope that seemed to extend to her waist. Perhaps it served as a signal of fertility in the same way an Isaurian's mating crest did. *Interesting.*

Youngest Brother took a deep breath to settle his nerves again and relax his slitted pupils. He touched his satchel once.

Embraced destiny.

YOUNGEST BROTHER APPROACHED the booth politely. Diffidence was too soft. Arrogance was likely to get him struck down by lightning bolts, like the others. Confidence without challenge, then. After all, he was uninterested in mating rights with the female. This was purely a business proposition.

The female watched him draw near with a single raised eyebrow. *How did humans do that?* She leaned closer to the wizard she was snuggled up against and whispered something in his ear. Up close, the wizard had a helmet of curly dark brown hair, cut short, and brown skin the color of fresh khave. He was dressed in pants and a short tunic of some strange material, with a jacket over it that was almost shiny.

The male also raised an eyebrow as he turned to look. *I must learn how they do that. It appears to be a human trick, perhaps a new language.*

Youngest Brother smiled, a gesture he hoped was

universal across all sentient races. He didn't get blasted by lightning, so it must be close enough to the human analog.

They stared at each other for a few heartbeats.

Youngest Brother decided to break the silence. "Do you read the ancient tongues?"

Both sets of human eyebrows went up. Youngest Brother flickered his inner eyelid, just to show that he had non-verbal communication methodologies as well. The wizard started, just the slightest bit.

The human scanned the crowd, over and behind Youngest Brother, obviously looking for signs of ambush. A bubble of near silence had emerged around them. Other patrons had not stopped to listen, but had shifted away and quieted, like herd animals just before a storm. A spook might trigger flight. The wizard was rightly feared this night.

The wizard noticed it as well. He leaned in to whisper something in the female's ear and palmed her a coin. She looked disappointed, but slid out of the booth.

The bar crowd parted as she made her way to bar. Youngest Brother shifted so he could keep one eye on the wizard and watch the female move with the other. The crowd seemed poised.

She nodded from the bar and picked up a pitcher of beer.

The wizard slid from the booth, eyed Youngest Brother, and pointed towards the female. "Follow me, please."

Youngest Brother skittered in the human's wake, aware that all noise had now ceased. Truly, the herd thought another storm imminent. He considered windows and other access points he might flee, given the risk.

The female, and then the wizard, passed the end of the giant wooden bar and entered a storage room with a rough table and a number of casks. Youngest Brother followed. The space smelled of dust and fermented grain.

He watched the wizard settle in a chair with his back to the door. The female deposited the pitcher on the table along with two glasses and stepped back. She pulled the door closed, leaving Youngest Brother alone with the wizard.

He was unsure if this was a wise way to end his quest. Or to begin it.

He stood perfectly still as the human studied him. It was an opportunity for him as well, broken though his scholar training had become.

The man finally reached out and poured fermented liquid into one of the mugs. He took a sip. "Which language did you have in mind?"

Youngest Brother paused, lost. *More than one?* He knew of draconic and the common tongue used in the villages and towns for trade. The one he spoke now with the human.

He felt the tip of his tongue slide the least amount out. He remembered humans and troglodytes blasted across the space of the bar by the wizard's eldritch bolts. He played a hunch. "I seek to translate some ancient scripts, but I do not know which language they represent."

The human leaned back in his chair, eyes glittering. Both hands were in view, but that meant nothing. He was a wizard. The silence hung. "Do you have a sample?"

Youngest Brother considered his mistake. If he took out the icon here, the wizard might kill him to steal it. But he had had nothing to scribe the words with, nor reason to do so.

He drew inspiration from the fermented grain beverage. He pointed. "May I?"

The wizards brows moved together. *Truly, Youngest Brother needed to learn that language. Perhaps the female would teach him.*

The wizard slid his chair back from the table a bit and gestured to the other chair.

Youngest Brother climbed onto the chair and reached across to the pitcher. He dipped a finger in the liquid and quickly drew one of the words he remembered onto the wooden surface.

The wizard leaned forward, focused intently. His own tongue tip appeared for the briefest hint.

The human reached inside his jacket and withdrew a small flat rectangle, perhaps two of Youngest Brothers' hands together in length, and more than one in width. He placed it on the table. A small wooden cylinder emerged to join it.

Youngest Brother smelled leather and leaves. So. A book. He had heard stories of such a thing, but his village was too poor to have such treasures. Teaching was oral down the generations, with writing reserved for a few scholars, such as himself.

The wizard flipped the book open. The pages were blank. Youngest Brother was disappointed. The wooden dowel was laid across the paper. "Here."

Youngest Brother considered the dowel. It appeared to

be hollow and contain a darker substance. He sniffed it carefully. Hmm. Coal graphite. It would leave a permanent mark on the vegetable substance. *What an useful invention!*

Youngest Brother took the writing device in one hand like a fork and pulled the book closer. Quickly, he scribed as many words and phrases as he could remember from the surface of the icon.

When he finished, he slid the book back to the wizard and rested on his haunches, suddenly tired from the psychic ordeal of his day.

He watched the wizard lift the book and flip randomly through the several marked pages.

The wizard made a strange whistling sound. Youngest Brother nearly fled.

The human stared at him intently. "You are a scribe, no?"

Youngest Brother chewed carefully on the word in his mind. It did not exist in Isaurian, though the roots were there. "I, sir, am a scholar."

The human grinned. At least it looked like a grin. The eyebrows did not move, so perhaps it wasn't. More things to ask the female.

The human laid the book on the table and pointed to one of the strings of symbols. "What you have, my little friend, is a map. This phrase means 'Kunlin Mountain Range' in the most-ancient dialect. It is a place south and west from here."

Youngest Brother put on a serious face, but inwardly, he giggled with delight. The legends were true. "I see. And what would you charge to translate the rest of the terms?"

He watched the human lean back in his chair and take a slow drink from the mug. The level of the fluid did not appear to alter appreciably. It felt like a game of dragon-chess with Eldest Brother. He comported himself accordingly.

Time passed.

The wizard leaned forward. "How about a different option?"

Youngest Brother attempted to cock his head at an angle, similar to the way he had seen the two humans interact. Apparently, it worked.

The human smiled and pointed at another word-string. "I am extremely interested in learning more about this map. This is the ancient word *depot*. It means a place where the ancients often stored weapons. Perhaps a few survive."

Youngest Brother's inner eyelid flickered. Shut. Open. He cursed such a loss of control before his negotiating foe.

The wizard apparently took it as a hopeful sign. "I propose a partnership. You and I. Your map. My... wizardry. Perhaps we recruit a few experts. Then we go see if there are any weapons there. Your thoughts?

Youngest Brother was almost too stunned to think. He sputtered. "But you are a wizard. Wizards do no put themselves at risk. They live in tall towers and research great thoughts."

The human smiled at him. "And they don't get into bar fights."

Youngest Brother made a moue. *True.* This one did not fit the pattern of wizards from the old tales. "Why would you do this thing?"

The human grew serious. One finger tapped the tabletop. "Many reasons. Wealth. Power. Knowledge. And I really don't like dragons."

Youngest Brother felt his toes tingle and try to curl under. Could this wizard be an ally against the great ones? It was true that the war between the great ones and the scaleless was ancient. The Sky Empire and the Empire Of The West had fought many wars. Only along the fringes were the lesser races able to carve out a kind of space between the elves and the troglodytes, and their overlords. And their gods.

He tried a different tack. "How would we pay for these *experts*? I have very little cash to hire people."

The man smiled. "Ah, but you have the map. It has the potential for great value. Among my kind, there is a term called *sweat equity*. I will contribute gold to the partnership. You will bring information. We will share the rewards equally."

Youngest Brother had never heard it called such a thing, but the poor villagers of his clan understood *barter*. From each according to his ability. To each according to his needs. "How do you know such things?"

The man took a real drink of his beverage this time. "Before I was a wizard, in a land far, far away, I was a merchant."

Youngest Brother shuddered at such a terrible disgrace. "What of your mate?"

The human cocked his head and raised an eyebrow. Again, the language of face muscles.

Youngest Brother suppressed the need to practice the

movements. "The female. Your consort. The one guarding our privacy."

"Ah. Irsh. Actually, I was considering hiring her to join us. She is a thief, not a prostitute, although she occasionally is mistaken for the latter."

Youngest Brother could not resist mirroring the cocked head. *Practice, of course.* "Why would a wizard need a thief? Is your magic insufficient?"

Youngest Brother braced for a lightning bolt, surprised by the sudden audacity of his tongue.

The human laughed. "Rarely. But she is a wonderful source of gossip. And occasionally, bad men need to have bad things happen to them."

"Only bad men?"

The human's smile grew immense. "Ethics, my little friend, are what you do when no one is looking."

The scaleless were weird. "I see. I believe such a partnership is acceptable. How shall we proceed?"

He watched the wizard move the pitcher and the mugs to the side and dry the tabletop with a sleeve. "Can I see the device?"

Youngest Brother felt his insides freeze solid. *How? But...* He prevaricated. "What device?"

The human pointed a finger at his satchel. "The one in your bag. I detected it with my...magic...when we entered the room."

Yes. Of course. A wizard. And yet... "But you did not take it. Even though you could have?"

The wizard grew very serious. "This planet will never advance, as long as the mighty terrorize the meek. An Isaurian rebel seeking dragon-slaying weapons is a cause I find noble. Which reminds me. What is your name, my friend?"

Youngest Brother remembered Eldest Brother's words about trusting the scaleless. "You could not pronounce it. Call me *Partner*."

"Very well, Partner. My full name is Doyle Iwakuma. You should call me Doyle."

Youngest Brother touched his first human as they shook hands across the scarred wood. Scaleless flash felt like fresh leather. It was strangely warm and vaguely moist. "That is a very strange name. Where are you from?"

The wizard, Doyle, smiled in a detached, knowing manner. "Farther away than could probably imagine, my friend."

Youngest Brother, *Partner*, nodded. "I see." He would, eventually, but could not have dreamed it that day.

THREE
TRAVAILS

"Remind me again, Partner, why we have to walk there?"

The warrior, Sachesu, enjoyed calling him by that name, even though his partnership was with the wizard Doyle and the warrior was an *employee,* to quote the wizard's odd term.

At nearly eight feet tall, the ogre was nearly three times Youngest Brother's height, and at least five times his mass. According to Doyle, the ogres were created by the first god, *Mustafa,* to provide overseers for the orcs, much as angels for the elves and pucks and dwarves, or troglodytes for his own kind. But this ogre treated Youngest Brother with respect and humor.

The human woman, Irshandra ("Call me Irsh.") did as well. It must be a custom among the scaleless. Wyverns and troglodytes would be jockeying with their own kind for edge and social stature constantly. Perhaps it was safe here because they represented three different species, plus a wizard?

Youngest Brother decided to attempt humor. It was a novel method of communication for him. Troglodytes were very literal. "Because the terrain is too rough for mounts, and ogres apparently cannot fly. This must have been an oversight obviously corrected when the gods made the angels and the wyverns, Sachesu."

The ogre turned to him with a look of stunned disbelief, met a grin, grinned back. The grin became laughter. "No, Partner, I am not a magus. Otherwise, I would be a king."

The female who-was-not-Doyle's-mate chimed in. "Just as well. You'd be a horrible king. I like him, Doyle. Very few people can make an ogre laugh."

Doyle crested a rise and looked out at the rough, semi-arid canyon climbing away from the group. "Sach, this looks like a good enough place to camp. Let's find some shelter. We've got about another day, day and a half, in front of us."

Youngest Brother, *Partner* now, watched the wizard pull out a scroll tube of maps from his pack as he settled on a nearby rock outcrop. Uncorked, one would find the seven pieces of parchment and vellum, laboriously copied from the icon's faces and projections, what Doyle had called a *nav beacon* in the ancient tongue.

Carefully, Doyle selected one sheet, slid the rest home, and unrolled it on the rock.

Partner grabbed the far edge to keep it flat and sat down to study the map, upside down from him. Not that he needed to. All the time he had spent transcribing images and runes from the icon had required that he memorize every facet on the map in its relation.

The canyon they traversed was an arroyo that existed on both the ancient map and on more current versions. According to the wizard, that meant it had not changed much in more than four thousand years, nor had the ancient volcanic tor that had been hollowed by the magic of the ancients. The insides would not change much for ten thousand more.

Getting there, however, and finding one of the entrances, would be troublesome.

Partner felt Irsh lean over his shoulder to look. "Where are we?"

Doyle studied the map, so Partner put a finger down, a little east of center. "Here."

She examined it for a moment more. "And the cave?"

He shifted his finger farther south and east, tracing the line of the ravine until it began to flatten out on a plateau. "Somewhere here. It may be buried and require excavation."

Sachesu joined now, lurking over everyone, careful to stay out of the afternoon light. "What if the dragons destroyed it?"

Doyle smiled up at him. "It's made of mithral steel, Sach. Among the dragons, breathing ice, fire, or poison gas won't even scratch it. Maybe one of the acid-spitters could do it, if he wanted to spend ten years at the task. And even then, he's more likely to destroy the rocks around it that the metal."

"And the whole thing is made of mithral?" The ogre's eyes lit up with greed. "How much?"

Doyle shrugged. "The ancients had great powers. Probably tons of it."

Irsh whistled. "Just to make a door."

Doyle gave her a serious look. "Probably a door wide enough to drive two wagons and teams of horses through, and a hallway beyond. They built on a grand scale."

Partner sighed. "How far we have fallen. Today, a sliver of such metal to make a tool or weapon costs more than my village would have earned in a year. We must fix this."

Doyle put a friendly hand on his shoulder. "We are, Partner. Small steps."

Sachesu, ever practical, cleared his throat in an announcing way. "Which reminds me. Partner, how well can you fight?"

Partner looked up at the gigantic warrior as if he had suddenly grown a tail. He looked down to check. "I am a scholar, a keeper of the oral histories. I have never fought."

"Thought not." The ogre reached into his pack and pulled out a tiny knife in a sheath. It was perhaps the length of his hand. He handed it to Partner.

Partner took the blade, as long as his cubit, and considered it scientifically. "I cannot use this, Sachesu, though I thank you for the effort. I would not know how to engage."

He tried to hand it back, but the ogre caught his hand and engulfed it in his huge paw. "You will need to learn, Partner. Someday, it may mean your life."

Sachesu delicately arranged Partner's fingers and hand

around the grip. Partner expected the giant to grind his bones, but the touch was feather light. "You hold it like that. Blade forward, parallel to the ground. You can stab or slash with it."

"But I am a scholar."

"All the better, Partner. Nobody would expect you to be dangerous. And you don't have to worry about the edge catching on bone. It's mithral steel, magically honed to a razor edge."

Sachesu carefully caught the tip of the sheath and removed it, leaving the silvery dagger bare.

Partner studied the metal, and his reflection in it. The value of the metal was immense. The friendship, even greater. "Thank you, Sachesu. I shall endeavor to be worthy."

Irsh leaned close to study the little dagger. "And I need to teach you to throw it properly."

Partner was aghast. "You can throw a knife?"

Nearby, he watched Doyle swallow a laugh before Irsh could wipe the shocked look from her face. She sputtered instead.

Doyle came to her rescue. "Indeed, Partner. But this is not the best place to learn. When we return to the lowlands where there are many more trees. Perhaps we can find you a cactus tomorrow."

Partner studied the blade again, contemplated a mechanism whereby he could use it as a thrown weapon. It would not fly like a rock, it would tumble. And it was not long enough to remain stable like an arrow or javelin. He felt like he was the butt of another practical joke, only this time from his companions instead of his brother. "I do not see how."

Irsh smiled. "Like this." She pulled a similar weapon from her own belt, flipped it over to hold the tip between fingers and threw it overhand.

Partner watched it tumble in a circle that ended with the blade driven hilt-deep into what appeared to be a desert hare, that had been sitting perfectly still, fifteen feet away.

It quivered for the briefest moment. The blade, not the rabbit.

Partner was ever-so-slightly daunted. "I see."

Perhaps the scaleless were more dangerous than he realized.

Or the quest was, and he was only now realizing it.

"SACHESU, PLEASE STAND PERFECTLY STILL."

Partner caught the ogre's eyes to reinforce the message, and then slowly moved clockwise around the giant warrior.

Sachesu froze in place. Only his eyes moved. And one eartip. "Yes, Partner?"

Partner examined a spot on the rockwall just ahead of Sachesu. He got down on his hands and knees and thrust his snout even lower to get a good view.

Behind him, Doyle called out. "Partner?"

Partner could hear the strain in the voice, echoing softly in the utter silence of the dry ravine. He rocked back onto his heels and rotated just his head to look back over a shoulder. "We appear to have arrived."

The wizard stopped the hand reaching for a map. "Oh?"

"Indeed. Sachesu is standing on a deadfall trap that will drop him into a hunting pit."

He heard the female from farther back. "How can you be sure, Partner?"

He smiled grimly. "Because it is the same kind my village used to use to capture large ungulates."

Partner considered the device again. He made a face as he thought about how to disarm it, then lit up with a smile. "Sachesu, thank you for helping me save your life."

The ogre barely even breathed. "Huh?"

Partner pulled the fine little dagger from his satchel and slid the tip into a tiny crack in the rocks until the tip stopped. "Sachesu, please take a long step backwards and to your left. Wizard Doyle, please grab his arm if he begins to slide into the earth. I believe I have disarmed the device, but there will be only one way to be sure."

Partner watched the giant meekly stride towards the others. As he did, there was an audible click followed by a quiet metallic thump. Partner smiled to the others with delight.

They all remained frozen in place.

Irsh moved to her left to get a better view. "Is it safe?"

Partner stood. He bent and used a finger to trace a perfectly straight line in the sandy dirt. "Perfectly, Lady Irsh. And if we are careful, we should be able to enter the burrow via this machine. How much rope do we possess?"

Doyle approached, working his way around the deadfall instead of crossing it.

Partner watched him pull a wand from his belt. It was a short, squat, stubby wand, perhaps more like a knobby book than a wand, once he thought about it for a moment.

Doyle made careful arcane passes in the continuing silence. "Huh. Completely non-magical."

Partner nodded at his partner. "Indeed, Doyle. It is entirely mechanical in nature. A very common design."

He squatted down and quickly sketched in the dirt, a machine with pulleys, gears, and plates.

Irsh had crept close enough to view. A finger pointed. "What are those?"

Partner glanced up. She was paying close attention. The ogre still had not moved. He lowered his voice a bit. "Those are the spears that would impale the creature falling into the trap."

She nodded. "I see. And how do we get down there safely?"

Partner pointed to the knife wedged into the trigger. "The drop is open. Only the mithral strength of the steel kept it from being sheared off and opening the pit. Once we remove the cotter pin, the way will open and we can climb down. There will be space. As I said, my own village used a similar device to catch large game animals."

A very quiet ogrish voice. "Is it safe, Partner?"

Partner stood and leaned to get a clear view. He pointed to the safe path. "Indeed, friend Sachesu. Please step there and join us."

Irsh turned to the wizard. "Doyle? What do you think?"

Doyle thought for a moment. "Good as any. Knew we were close. Hopefully these caves connect to the place we're looking for. Let's do it."

She nodded and pulled her backpack off. Rope appeared, as did a lantern with a magical, ever-glowing stone. A cloak with a strange, almost shifting pattern of subtle colors, draped across her shoulders.

Irsh added a bandolier with several small knives protruding next. More knives got tucked into boots, belt, and a small one tucked inside of the gap her cleavage produced in her armored shirt. More were added to bracers on both wrists, suggesting ambidexterity in a manner Partner found most unsettling.

These people below were his kind. Obviously, they would welcome visitors, wouldn't they?

He grew further unsettled as Doyle checked several esoteric magic items of likely offensive and defensive capabilities. Sachesu dug a blue buckler the size of Partner's chest from his backpack and strapped it on his wrist, along with a helmet that had a magically glowing gem set in the forehead.

Had he signed up for a small war? "Friend Doyle, is all this warlikeness necessary? Can we not negotiate with the local tribe for their assistance?"

The wizard looked down at him confused for a moment. "Partner, many of the tribes in these hills do not consider it cannibalism to eat humans and ogres."

"Truly?"

Partner was intrigued at such behavior. So unlike his

now-lost village. And his scholarly training was intrigued. *What did ogre taste like, anyway?* He shrugged.

Partner checked his satchel and adjusted the scabbard of his little knife on his belt, just to fit in with his more-bellicose associates. "Are we in readiness?"

Each nodded in turn.

Partner gripped the little knife and pulled.

Nothing happened.

He pulled again.

The blade remained stubbornly wedged in place.

Hmph.

"Sachesu, may I impinge upon your greater musculature to withdraw the weapon from the blocking mechanism?"

The ogre stepped close and leaned over. *Garlic and pepper breath.*

A paw engulfed the blade.

Nothing moved.

The ogre looked up and whistled. "This will take some work. It is in there tight."

Sachesu paused, seated himself, and braced a foot against the stone wall. Both hands gripped and pulled with a growl.

The blade popped clear.

The trapdoor hinged open with a silent suddenness.

Sachesu began to tumble over backwards into the fifteen foot drop. Partner flopped awkwardly across the ogre's shin guards, pinned the ankles down until he could put a hand down and stop his fall.

"Whoa."

Partner was unsure who spoke. Both Doyle and Irsh looked into the revealed pit.

Rows of two-foot-long spears set into the floor rusted in the dry air, like rotting teeth.

Sachesu lifted Partner to his feet and stood. "Thank you, Partner. What do we think?"

Doyle turned to them with an ominous stare. "Looks like the mouth of hell."

FOUR
UNDERGROUND

PARTNER CONSIDERED the tunnel's dimensions, decided it must have been cut for humans. *Cut?* Yes, the walls were perfectly straight and cleanly smooth, with an arching peak. Sachesu was able to walk down the center without ducking. His own kind would have made warrens with four foot ceilings. Troglodytes would have preferred narrower walls. Wyverns would have made them wider.

And the magic down here was palpable.

Strips set flush into the roof glowed with a sharp, white light as they approached, and then faded after they passed. It was so unlike sunlight as to make his scales turn almost mint-colored. The air had a clean, post-rain feel that suggested magically-powered fans pushing it around, rather than the stale musk of his home caverns

But no people.

No dust covered the floor to raise footprints. No spiders wove webs in corners, but there were no insects either.

"Wizard Doyle, I have a question that requires your experience with magic to grasp."

Up front, at the head of the their little column, Doyle paused and stepped back around Sachesu's massive bulk. Behind, Partner glanced and saw Irsh take a few steps away to drift into the dusky darkness.

"Yes, Partner? What's on your mind?"

Partner pointed at the upper edge of a nearby wall. "Since we have descended into the earth, I have seen no other creatures besides ourselves, including the basest insects. I would have expected…something."

He watched the wizard pull another magical device, the shape and size of a large, flat river stone, from his belt and hold it in the air, making passes like a priest sprinkling holy water on the faithful. The ritual magic was utterly fascinating. It felt like home.

Partner suppressed a pang of longing.

Doyle finished his ritual and returned the item to a belt pouch. "Interesting. Partner, you're correct. I can detect no other *lifeforms* beyond ours."

Lifeforms? "Lifeforms, wizard Doyle?"

The human smiled wryly. "One ogre, two humans, one isaurian. Nothing else as far as I can scan."

Scan? The scaleless were weird enough, wizards just made it worse.

Irsh appeared at a silent jog, lights flickering on and off as she moved. She paused as she came even. "Someone coming. Behind us."

Partner turned with the rest. He could hear a strange hissing rumble in the sudden quiet, but no ceiling lights marked the creature's progress.

He watched fascinated as Doyle pulled a vial from his belt and twisted it without breaking the material. Something popped. Two good shakes to mix the contents and it began to softly glow. "How it that done, Doyle?"

The human glanced down, grinned, and snapped the vial down the hallway with a hard underhanded toss. "Alchemy."

"Ah. Of course."

Downrange, the glowing vial tumbled to a halt. It waited forlornly in a small puddle of yellow-green light. It was not lonely for long.

A creature emerged from the darkness. Partner thought of a giant land tortoise, but this creature traveled on what appeared to be black wheels instead. It rolled to a stop a few feet short of the glowing vial and appeared to consider it for several seconds.

Doyle reacted first. "Oh, crap. Everyone run. This way."

The human took off at a jog away from the creature. Partner followed, aware of how dangerous tortoises were on the surface to his kind. Behind, he heard Sachesu begin to trot. Irsh never made a sound when she moved.

The ogre called softly as he caught up, long loping strides more than making up for Doyle's headstart. "Doyle, what was that thing?"

Doyle glanced back, but kept his attention forward. He seemed hard pressed to find the right word as Partner watched. "Call it a golem. Close enough."

Partner was even more fascinated. "A golem? Really? How exciting!"

Doyle kept moving. "Sure, if you think an immortal,

nearly-unkillable machine designed to keep things out of these tunnels is fun. We need to outrun it."

Partner was deeply pained. "I am a scholar, not an athlete. This is the greatest speed I can attain. If need be, you should sacrifice me to protect the others."

Sachesu swooped up close. "Your pardon, Partner. Can't do that."

The ogre grabbed him around the waist and lifted him into the air, much as an adult would carry an infant. It was extremely efficient, if a bit demeaning.

Immediately, the group began moving at a greater clip.

Partner took advantage of his vantage point to study the tunnel. "Doyle, we are approaching another of those strange sliding doors that you referred to as an *blast barrier* before. If the creature is intent on pursuing us, perhaps we could seal that door and use your magic to disable the mechanism, thereby trapping it here?"

They continued to run.

Doyle pulled up as he crossed the line carved in the metal floor. "Irsh, see if you can find a lock we can seal. I don't want to trap ourselves in on the wrong side if we don't have to."

Sachesu paused and set Partner carefully down. "Is that thing really unkillable, Doyle?"

The wizard explored one wall as Irsh took the other side of the hall. "That model is extremely rugged. It was built to keep the tunnels clear of debris and do basic maintenance."

Partner considered the term. *Model?* That suggested many of them rather than a single demon made metallic flesh, such as the wyverns always threatened to conjure. *Interesting.*

Irsh punched a button triumphantly. "Got it."

The door rattled closed with a hiss and a bang. Irsh continued to address strangely colored magical runes that glowed in the wall at human height.

Partner could not make sense of the colors nor the strange writing, but something was happening. He felt his ears suddenly pop. "What is that feeling?"

Irsh shrugged. "I learned that trick on a set of ruins in the human lands. It keeps the door from being opened by someone on the other side."

Partner considered it. "I see. But why do my ears feel stiff?"

Doyle inspected the panel closely. "Overpressure. Sealed against gas attacks so the atmosphere is charged as a defense mechanism."

Partner recognized the words. Each of them. They even strung together nicely. They still made no sense. He paused to consider them some more.

Doyle seemed satisfied with the runes. "It will hold for now. We need to move quickly. I'm not sure how smart the...golem is."

Sachesu approached politely. "Partner, my apologies for before. Would it acceptable to convey you at speed again?"

Partner blinked both sets of eyelids in surprise. *Ogres didn't have manners. All the tales agreed on that point. But still.* "Of course, Sachesu. Thank you."

It was only proper. Death might still be on their heels.

IT WAS ANOTHER DOOR. Another closed *blast barrier* blocked their path. Two others had surrendered to Irsh's patient and nimble fingers and been sealed up again behind them. Doyle seemed excited that the magic controlling them was still intact after so long.

Partner was not sure he shared the human's enthusiasm. Dragons were also immortal.

He joined a kneeling Doyle to study one of the hand-drawn maps. The wizard had augmented this one extensively from what he called the *standard design architecture* of the ancients. It showed a warren of perfectly straight lines intersecting perfect arcs of a circle, like a student's lesson in geometry. So unlike his own kind.

Partner considered the tunnels they had traversed to this point. One cave-in had blocked them, but a side tunnel had been available after a short backtrack. More recently, the tunnels were more poorly lit and dusty, so perhaps the golem was unable to pursue them thus. By now, they should be reaching close to the center of the mountain.

The sound of Irsh's palm slapping the metallic panel in disgust got everyone's attention. Partner was unsure of the word that accompanied it, although he suspected it was one impolite for proper company. He did not press her to repeat it.

Doyle stood and stretched. "Locked?"

She shrugged eloquently. "The magic has been dispelled. There is damage to the wall, so maybe an earth-shift has broken something. I can't get it to do anything."

Doyle smiled and approached. Partner ghosted along in his wake.

Partner watched the wizard draw out his little divination tool from his belt again and cast some spell on the door. Nothing happened, regardless of the gestures employed, so Partner was inclined to agree with the blade-throwing female.

Doyle joined their conclusion. "Yup. Dead. Good thing you brought along a wizard. Hopefully, we can get the casing open and locate a *manual override* or *crosswire* the *primary power supply*. Let me take a look."

Partner had learned that the wizard frequently fell into a very strange arcane cant when he worked. He sometimes recognized words from the ancient tongue, and was learning a tremendous amount. The troglodyte masters and their wyvern overlords would be doomed if he could find the tools to fight them, especially the fire wands they used to kill and destroy from range.

Doyle pulled a strangely-shaped instrument from another pouch on his belt. It was round, like a crowbar, with a flat tip at one end, but only a human hand long. The other end had a strange, crystalline grip.

Partner was puzzled, until he watched Doyle fit the chisel tip into a small slot in one corner and twist. Something moved. As the wizard twisted more, a round piece of metal rose out of a hole.

When the little metal cylinder fell free, Partner's inner eyelids flickered. *Magic! The darkest arts.*

Doyle moved on to another corner of the lock and found a second slot. Partner realized that each corner had such a slot. Each surrendered to the wizard's patient hands.

Partner held his breath as Doyle removed the last slotted cylinder. The entire face of the lock came free with a twist of the chisel-tip. Doyle handed it down to Partner, standing so patiently quiet next to him. "Partner, could you set this down for me? I need to get to the innards of the lock."

Partner rested this new icon on the floor well away from their feet and studied the strange locking mechanism. It had no gears or pullies. Instead, the interior was a strange green color, with bumps and shapes in other colors, and golden threads binding it all together.

Doyle looked down. "Careful. It's about to get dusty."

Partner flicked his inner eyelids closed as the human took a breath and blew sharply into the device. For good measure, he closed his nostrils as well. It was just as well. There was a great deal of dust. Apparently, the land tortoise was entirely absent.

As the dust passed, Partner studied the device. The golden threads were marred near one corner. He pointed without touching. "Friend Doyle, has the device been damaged by an insect?"

Doyle leaned down to get a better view. He muttered a spell and pointed his right index finger, just as he had at the bar that night. This time, a white light appeared where he pointed.

Partner was thrilled. It was a different spell than the one he had cast before. Partner might yet learn the arcane arts, given enough time.

Doyle stuck his left hand closed and rubbed at the damaged spot. "Good eyes, Partner. Something took a bite of the *plastic* before deciding it didn't like the taste."

Partner smiled at the compliment. "It is reparable?"

He watched the human trace the golden threads both directions with a finger while muttering more arcanums under his breath. Doyle worked his way down to a silver circle in the opposite corner that he tapped. "Hmm."

Partner shifted himself a little to the side to watch unobtrusively as the wizard took off his backpack and pulled out a wrapped leather satchel and unwound it on the floor. Inside were all manner of small metal tools, many looking like alien insects frozen and then cast.

The human picked one that ended in a strange circular claw and measured it against the silver circle. With more muttering, he brought the claws to life and pressed them forward.

Partner watched rapt as the claws seemed to sniff at the thing and slowly embrace it, flowing and molding themselves into small gaps and biting down. Never had he imagined *magic* like this. Perhaps his kind should have more travels to the lands of the scaleless.

After several moments, all of the claws had achieved purchase. They seemed to all pull at the same moment and the silver circle popped free to reveal the cylinder as a disk two fingers across and a fingernail thick.

As Doyle withdrew the magical metal creature, the claws lost their grip and the disk fell, Partner's hand flashed out and snatched it out of the air, much like an errant insect. It was extremely cool to the touch. The back was a smooth black material that was neither metal nor wood, inset with two smaller metal disks that seemed to be made of gold.

He presented it on an open palm. "Doyle?"

The wizard reached down carefully to pick it up. "Thank you, Partner. You seem to be good luck."

Irsh piped up at that moment. "We knew that. Hey, Doyle? Are we likely to be here for a while?"

Partner watched the human weigh the costs of his magic carefully. They were in a dead end, if something like the iron turtle came, but this was also possibly the last door before the innermost nest of the mountain.

Doyle looked up from the thing he held. "Maybe an hour, if I can fix this."

She cocked her head at him. "What's an hour?"

"Sorry. Long enough to fix some food and some tea, or take a nap, but not longer than that."

She walked up behind the ogre and began rifling through his oversized pack. "Tea, coming up. And some flatcakes with jam."

Partner crossed his ankles and sat to watch the wizard at work. So much to learn.

DOYLE SNAPPED the little silver disk from some strange new device with one hand as he sipped tea with the other. He handed it back to the strange silver insect and pressed it against the lock device.

It writhed for a moment, and then settled with a loud click.

Partner's inner eyelid flickered with delight.

He watched the wizard trace the golden threads back to the previously-marred corner that had been repaired with new threads Doyle carried in his tool satchel.

A small green light flickered to life, happy, in the center of the thing.

Doyle smiled. "And it will hold a charge. Not sure how long, but we should be good."

Partner understood every word the human spoke, and not one meaning. It must be awkward to be so far removed from everyday people concerns.

Doyle pressed a finger against a large red circle in one corner while muttering. The words seemed to be profanities instead of arcana, but sometimes it was hard to differentiate.

Nothing happened for a moment, and then a faint grinding sound was audible.

Partner leapt to his feet as the large door, the *blast barrier*, moved. But it only traveled a few inches before it froze in place. Doyle muttered more arcana. Or profanities.

Partner leaned close to the opening and sniffed at the slight breeze coming out. It smelled more like home than these tunnels had. Earthy. Warm. Lizardy. And dragon. Perhaps the adventure had truly just begun.

Behind him, he heard the wizard raise his voice to conversational levels. "Sach, we'll need your crowbar and muscles now."

The ogre laughed. "Nobody ever loves me for my mind."

Irsh laughed as well. "Perhaps you should take up philosophy then."

Sachesu's laugh boomed. "The world is not prepared for an ogre of letters. Remind me when we get home. Your pardon, Partner. Oversized thug must earn his pitiful keep now."

Partner stepped back with a grin to watch as the giant wedged the tip of a monstrous chunk of black metal into the gap. The crowbar easily outweighed him, but Sachesu handled it like a wand. Sachesu leaned into the tool with a grunt.

The door moved another two handspans before it stopped.

Partner watched Doyle reach into his pack and pull out a small metal cylinder colored a rich blue, with a strange red crown. He shook the vial a few times and stepped close to the door near the center. Doyle pressed the crown and unleashed a small spray of a golden-brown fluid that flowed into the door jamb. It smelled of the strange coal brought up from the deepest mines.

Doyle stopped and looked up. "Try it now, Sach."

The ogre took a deep breath and flexed. The door suddenly slid several feet before binding. Even dropping the crowbar and pushing directly in the gap, Sachesu could not move it. "Looks like that's it."

Doyle carefully returned the small sprayer to his belt. "Good enough. What's on the other side?"

Partner had stepped through, even as Sachesu had tried to move the door, the benefit of being small. The far side was dark. The floor was several inches higher, covered in smooth dirt that smelled old and stale. Partner knelt down and dug with one finger to confirm his suspicion. Underneath he found the same silver-white metal hallway that his companions had been traversing.

Partner touched a wall as well. It was the same metal as

well, but covered in dirt and oily grime, as through years of oil lamps had left their smoky deposit. Or perhaps centuries. The air had that kind of dead, stale smell to it.

There was also darkness. The ceiling lights that had magically activated and faded as he had moved were absent here. Covered? Damaged? Removed? He would need the ogre's great height and Doyle's magical lamp to be sure. It was good to have useful friends. He heard them arrive behind him.

Irsh was apparently first through the gap. Her lamp was barely enough to augment what came through. "Partner?"

He turned, aware that the light would glow off his inner eyes. Even in his mind, the words sounded ominous. "We must exercise great care, Irsh."

He watched her unconsciously touch one of the many knives on her left wrist. "Why is that, Partner?"

The others joined them as he spoke. "There is a dragon in these tunnels."

The lighter-skinned, red-haired Irsh paled. Doyle's skin took on a grayer pallor as Partner watched. "Are you sure?"

Partner nodded. He had seen the signs in his companions before, but this confirmed it. "It is an unmistakable smell. Perhaps too subtle for your kinds, but obvious to mine. Fortunately, he has not been in this part of the warren in a very long time. Perhaps since he was very young, and much smaller."

Irsh sniffed hard. "I smell…something. Can you tell the color? And are you sure it is male?"

Partner shook his head. "I can only presume. Most dragons are male. The Great Mother, *Ailaendae*, the First

Dragon, designed the lizard races to have a very different gender balance from the scaleless."

Sachesu looked confused. "The scaleless?"

A human would have blushed. Partner felt his scales flare out from his skin in embarrassment. "My apologies, Sachesu. It was an impolite term my kind uses to describe those children of the First God, *Mustafa*, that he chose to make in his own image. Unlike lizardkind. Scaleless. As a philosopher, is there a better term to use?"

Sachesu paused. "I do not know, Partner. We tend to call everyone humanity, to reflect our common heritage. Though I do not know how many races can cross-breed, beyond the half-elves who are commonly mules. I will give this thought."

Partner flattened his scales down, redeemed in the knowledge that he was a friend of the first great ogre philosopher, as far as he knew. Truly, the world was changing.

Doyle reached up and pulled a gem on a gold chain from his tunic, revealing the edge of a mail shirt underneath. He touched the back once and the gem began to glow with a soft white glow. "Partner, I think you should lead, since you have the best nose. The chambers we seek should be close."

Partner felt his face grow serious. "Indeed, Doyle."

He moved to the center of the dirty-covered hallway and contemplated the darkness. There was a dragon in these tunnels. A dragon he intended to kill.

FIVE
THE DRAGON'S DEN

PARTNER FOUND the smell almost overwhelming. The air seemed to hang with a taste he thought he could chew, earthy and lizardy all at once. Dragonmusk.

He crept along a small side hallway, carved by his own kind, rather than the ancients or the troglodytes. The signs were there. A smooth finish to three feet, and then rougher to a ceiling eight or nine feet overhead, perhaps four or six inches narrower at the top than the bottom. Textured floors cut with shallow grooves on each side of the tunnel to channel any water to the edges and away from walking feet.

Troglodyte tunnels tended to be perfectly square vertically, and lack the drain channel, since they never had to clean after any flood or springleak. They also moved in straight lines, rather than following natural seams in the stone.

After nearly a day in the tunnels of the ancients, this tunnel felt cramped, where he would have once called it homelike. And it smelled strange. Old. Forgotten. Stale. But the dragonmusk was strong.

Partner stopped and took a deep breath. He had never smelled dragonmusk before, but his mind knew the flavor. Perhaps Ailaendae had programmed it into her followers when she made them. Dragonfear. Partner settled his scales and took another two steps to a soft corner.

His nose detected a breeze blowing toward him. The musk was stronger now. Perhaps even enough for Doyle or Sachesu to smell it and understand. He must be close. He peeked around.

He felt his inner eyelids flicker uncontrollably for a second.

Below, an image made him want to fall to his knees in worship.

Partner barely stopped himself from crying out in sudden ecstasy. Below him, looking down from the ledge he found himself on, stretched out on the warm sands, lay a tremendous dragon, resplendent blue scales glowing in lamp light.

A voice whispered in his ear, unbidden.

It persisted, demanded attention, worship. It overawed his mind, except for one little corner that cataloged the entire affair scientifically, and another corner that complained loudly at such effrontery.

The dragon captured him, unknowing.

Another voice intruded. A different voice. Quiet. Pleading. Penetrating. The awake parts of his mind responded impotently. The rest continued to venerate.

Something intruded on his breathing. Insistent.

Something wrapped around his nostrils, blocked them shut. Tried to choke him.

Partner turned to look at what was attacking him, found Irsh hovering silently beside him, one hand pinching the end of his snout. *How long had he been frozen?*

She looked a question at him, concern written on her features. The language of face muscles he had been learning from her.

Partner understood, nodded.

She released the grip on his nose, put a finger to her lips to indicate silence, and moved deeper into the caverns, where the rest waited. A thoroughly-chastened Isaurian scholar followed.

Around several curves and safely removed, Doyle and Sachesu rested. Doyle held one of his Witchfinder artifacts in one hand, studied the ebb and flow of the arcana under this mountain. Sachesu sipped cold tea from a flask and appeared to think philosophical thoughts. At least, that was what the ogre had taken to telling everyone.

Doyle looked up. "We were beginning to get worried."

Partner felt all of his scales flare in embarrassment again. "It is worse than I imagined. When the Great Mother made the lizard races, she programmed dragonfear and dragonworship into us. I saw him, wizard Doyle, the wyrm who is the overlord of these tunnels, and wanted nothing more than to worship him. I could watch it in my mind, but not fight it."

Irsh joined him as he sat. She touched his shoulder with a friendly hand. "Can you breathe through your mouth?"

Partner felt his mind upend. "Can I what?"

She persisted. "Your mouth. Could you breathe if your nostrils were blocked?"

Partner nodded, unsure at the line of questioning.

Irsh smiled. "Because when I found you, your nostrils were flared open as far as they could go and you were snorting like a horse. You said the power is in the smell. So we need to ruin your sense of smell for a while."

Partner-the-scholar laughed with delight in his mind. Partner-the-dragon-worshipper wanted to go back. Partner-the-adventurer voted against the addiction. "Very good. How do we do such a thing?"

He watched her pull a length of cloth and a vial of unknown liquid from an inner pocket. "With a blindfold for your nose."

Truly, the scaleless were weird, but it was good to have interesting friends.

PARTNER WATCHED the door surrender to Irsh's patient fingers. She was getting better at finding the combinations that caused the ancient magic to surrender. The silence was welcome, if deafening, broken only by the slight hiss of wind passing through the tunnel as the door opened.

Irsh blew out a long breath. "About time."

Partner sat close, absorbing everything he could about the ancient arcana, the *technology*, that he could. His nose blindfold made him feel awkward and silly-looking if he stopped to think about it. He chose to abstain from philosophical concerns. "Problems, Lady Irsh?"

She glanced down. "Wasn't sure I could crack that one."

Partner cocked his head. "It seemed to go quickly."

She nodded. "Yes, but the last several have used the same combination of *buttons*. This one was an older code, what Doyle called the *primary reversion default setting*. Luckily, it worked here."

Partner nodded sagely. "Luckily, we have an expert."

Doyle joined them as the door finished sliding to the left and disappearing into the wall. He whistled. "Isn't that interesting."

Partner looked past the threshold. The room revealed was different that the dragon's tunnels outside. The walls were the silver-white they had been in the first caves, including the floor. Inside, the ancient, magical lights flickered suddenly to life.

Partner started to step forward, diligent in his task as scout, but Irsh held him back. "A few moments, Partner. The air in there is very stale and smells strange."

Partner turned to her with an impish smile, nose still *blindfolded* with the stinky cloth. "All air is currently strange, Irsh."

She laughed quietly. "Okay. More so.

Behind him, Doyle's voice became sharp.

Partner did not recognize any of the astonished profanities, only the tone. "Wizard Doyle?"

He glanced back as the human gulped. "Those are original shipping containers."

Partner understood the context of the words, if not the words themselves. Something brought to this world by the gods when they first fled the motherworld. Unbelievably ancient artifacts, lost and forgotten, locked away in a chamber that could not be opened. One hand strayed to his satchel, psychically touching the great icon inside. He paused to genuflect mentally.

Irsh paused a few more moments, although Partner reflected that her wait was pragmatic, rather than religious. She rose, sniffed carefully, and stepped into the room. The others followed.

Inside, Partner recognized many of the magic runes, what Doyle called *letters*, on the sides of the boxes. He could even recognize some of the words thus formed, having studied them and asking the wizard as they had transcribed the great map from the icon.

He considered the great azure wyrm, apparently asleep in the levels above, as well as the burning remains of his village. "Wizard Doyle, I have a request."

The human looked up from a stack of small cubes tucked into one corner. "Yes, Partner?"

Partner forced the words past a suddenly tense, rebellious jaw. "Which of these will slay a dragon?"

Partner-the adventurer felt his heart race and dread shoot a spurt of hot acid fire into his stomach. Partner-the-dragon-worshiper screamed with dismay in his head. Strong psychic pain wrapped painful hot tentacles around the base of his skull and squeezed, as if punishing his apostasy. Both hands clenched into painful fists. He would have fallen but for Sachesu's mountain-like hand suddenly there to hold him.

The ogre squatted down with concern. "Partner?"

He blinked past the pain. "We were programmed to deify them, Sachesu."

The ogre nodded perceptively. "I understand, my friend. Becoming something greater than the gods intended can be a painful awakening."

Partner nodded silently.

Greater than the gods intended.

SIX

AWAKENING

A NOSTRIL TWITCHED. It was a minor thing, but it heralded wakefulness from slumber.

An eyelid opened next. Just the light-blocking lid, not the flying lid nor the inner-most lid. It cracked halfway, as it to examine the great room.

Nothing was amiss. But still, something had roused him.

The other eye opened. Both came fully open as his dream faded.

Marasem lifted his great azure head from his clawed hands and delicately sniffed the breeze.

Breeze? He was hundreds of feet underground, several awkward turns from sunlight. There should be no breeze.

And yet, there was the faintest one. That was enough to wake him, something new after six hundred and forty three years in this nest. But it did not explain his dismay.

He took a deeper lungful.

There. Human-smell. Ogre-smell.

Invaders.

Someone had snuck into his mountain while he slept. Past his guards, his wyverns, his *machines*. He had been violated. Had the Sky Empire finally decided to renew the war they lost so long ago? Would he need to rouse his brothers? Alert the Empire of the West? Perhaps visit the Great Mother herself?

Such news might improve his breeding stock even more at the next flight.

Marasem sniffed again, tasted these two humans and the ogre that accompanied them.

So. Just scouts, perhaps. At most. More likely thieves. He had many treasures left over from the time when humans alone walked this world. Before *Mustafa* made the lesser bipeds. Before *Ailaendae*, the Great Mother, created wyrmkind. Before history itself.

He turned his great skull and looked back over his right shoulder. There. A ledge overlooking his nest. Had they been spying on him as he slept?

The great wyrm thought back to the founding of his nest. Those tunnels were among the oldest. They had been sealed off from an even-older base when the humans had been driven east-over-mountains. They had somehow found a way through the guardians on the far side and slipped into the back of his fortress.

Who to task? Which of his troglodytes did he trust enough to explore those back chambers, so close to his treasure vaults? None of the wyverns would do. Too much risk of a palace coup. No, he needed one young and ambitious, but not so stupid as to challenge Marasem himself.

Exhane? No, he had already been eaten for his audacity. Had it truly been three decades? Pity. He would have been useful today.

Wuaox, then? Simple, direct, brutal. Tireless. He could chase down a band of thieves and bring them to heel. Yes. It would be nice to hunt men again.

Marasem bellowed for his soldiers as he rose and made his way out of the warm sand pit to the audience chamber where he held court.

SEVEN

STEALING FIRE FROM THE GODS

DOYLE RESTED on his heels and watched. "Okay, repeat it one more time so I am confident you have it down."

Partner tasted the rhythms in his mind, etching them into deepest memory. In his hands, he cradled a short, stout weapon of the ancients. It was his own height, yet remarkably light, made from the magical alloy Doyle called *polymer*. It had a matte black finish, like one of the venomous tunnel vipers that occasionally plagued his village if surprised while hunting rodents.

Partner was sure it had grown warm to his touch, but is he moved a hand, it cooled almost instantly. Partner-the-scholar kept one hand in constant motion as an experiment.

He took a deep breath and began the chant. "This is a fire lance. It contains *ammunition* for three bolts. Each bolt is sufficient to slay any creature up to *Mark 9 face-tempered armour plate*. To arm the lance, the latch is slid open here."

Nimble fingers caressed a pair of buttons, pinched, and pulled them rearward. The lower center of the lance suddenly parted like a fresh chicken egg into two matched halves. Partner eyed the silver and black magical disk at his feet. He lifted it and slid it carefully but forcefully into the gap and felt the lance pull itself closed, as it alive and hungry for murder.

Partner fell into his rhythm again. "Once charged, the weapon seals and arms. The *safety* is right-handed, and located high on the human thumb side when held to fire."

He lifted the artifact and rested it to his shoulder, awkwardly, since his bones were not human, but it was close enough to a fit, according to the wizard. "The fire-lance is brought to the right shoulder, settled firmly against the cheek, and armed. Spot the target through the *heuristic optics* and center the cross, offsetting for *heat-induced shimmer* when engaging at great range."

His thumb found the safety by stretching as far as he could. He moved his hand off the safety, as Doyle had instructed while learning, and mimicked the press down to arm. His hand moved back into position inside the inner ring of the *trigger*, one of the few metal places he could touch. "An Isaurian must use two fingers to pull the trigger, to make up for the lesser travel of the device from safe to fire and smaller hands. The recoil is *backward-vented and minimal,* and the fire-lance returns to the ready position one heartbeat later."

Partner turned to eye the wizard hopefully. "*Ready to disarm?*"

Doyle smiled. "Very well done, Partner. Normally, it

would take a *recruit* half a day to learn that ritual. It took you three passes. I'm impressed."

Partner sniffed at his partner. "I am a scholar. We do not have books to remember things for us, so we must remember it for each other."

Sachesu laughed. "You must teach me these tricks, Partner. I was completely lost."

Partner nodded at the ogre, very serious. "Indeed, friend Sachesu. We must make you a scholar as well."

Across the way, Irsh corked her bottle of tea and rose from her seat on the floor. Her backpack was crammed with one of the smaller boxes. "Doyle, do we really have to leave most of this here?"

The wizard nodded. "Unfortunately, yes. While we could empty the boxes of the treasure, having the treasure containers makes them worth several times as much. What I plan to do is get back to town and arrange for us to have a couple of wagons, teamsters, and some sledges we can haul down here to properly loot the place. You have no idea what I could sell this stuff for, back home."

Partner's ear stubs perked up. "Where is home, friend Doyle? I have met many species on my adventure, but I have never seen a human with skin so dark brown as yours. Most humans, such as Irsh, are so pale as to be a faded pink."

He watched the human struggle with an answer. "I was born in a city known as Ithome in what you would call the kingdom of Ballard. It is so very far away from here, into the rising sun, that you would not comprehend the distances involved."

Sachesu's face grew serious. "East across the sea?"

Doyle nodded. "As good a term as any."

Irsh pointed. "So why does he get to take a firelance himself?"

Doyle started to reply, but Partner cut him off. "Because the map that led us here belonged to my village, before the wyverns destroyed my kin. The fire lance is my price for the rest."

Irsh's eyes blinked in a human version of surprise. Even Partner-the-scholar quailed a little at the fierce determination in his voice. Eldest Brother would be absolutely aghast at what he had turned into. But, hopefully, proud.

The War For Eternity was about to begin, led by the smallest Isaurian.

EIGHT
ESCAPE

PARTNER LOOKED UP interested as Sachesu shaded his eyes to get a better view. "Doyle, can I borrow your far-seeing artifact? We might have company."

Heads instantly rotated to the south. Doyle reached into his over-stuffed backpack and pulled out a small rounded box, made of the magical *polymer*, with a place for eyes to rest on one side and a large glass lens on the other. He handed it wordlessly to the ogre and helped Irsh the rest of the way out of the pit.

Sachesu studied the distant hillside and whistled. "Yes, they've definitely seen us and are coming this way."

Irsh let go of the rope as she made it to solid ground. "Can we outrun them?"

The giant handed the magic lenses back to Doyle. "Maybe. They appear to be on foot, so an infantry column."

Doyle stuffed the *binoculars* away and started moving

north. "If we can get to cover, we can try to lose them in the trees.

Sachesu nodded. "Agreed. Partner, would it be acceptable if I carried you for the first distance?"

Partner grabbed his satchel tightly and relaxed as he stepped into the ogre's grip. The fire lance strapped across his back made his balance feel strange. "Certainly, friend. Let us escape."

Sachesu set off at a soft jog, his long legs forcing Irsh and Doyle to almost run to keep up. "Partner, how fast can troglodytes move?"

Partner considered the many factors involved. He had never worked with humans before, so he only had stories and legends as he contemplated the dark line on the distant hillside pointed this way. "Over a short distance, I believe they can run faster, Sachesu, but it is an explosive movement that cannot be sustained over any great period. We should be able to make it to the trees well ahead of them and then hopefully disappear."

The trio set off at a ground-eating jog, glancing back occasionally. The column of troops continued to point right at them like an arrow of doom.

PARTNER HEARD a sound above the pounding of feet and looked to the sky. He felt his mind go, again, as the iridescent blue scales caught the afternoon light.

Partner-the-dragon-worshiper sighed happily inside. Partner-the-scholar studied the complex interplay of muscles and physics and marveled that the creature swooping in from behind had been designed and built from human stock originally, as had all intelligent creatures in the world. Partner-the-adventurer cried out, but he was pushed into a quiet corner by the dragon-worshiper and left silent and impotent.

Partner-the-adventurer pushed hard against the chains binding his mind. He railed. He raged. He kicked and bit and clawed. He howled profanities he had learned from Doyle, and Irsh, and even the great ogre philosopher, Sachesu.

A whisper escaped his constricted throat. "Dragon."

Sachesu glanced down as he loped along. "What was that, Partner?"

The ogre's words created an opening in the sheet of glass separating Partner from the outside world. In his mind, he stuck a finger into that hole and pulled, stretching it wider and tearing with all his might as he fought to pull himself through it and escape the trap built there by the Great Mother.

He took a breath across a suddenly dry mouth. He swallowed hard. The words came out almost audible. "Dragon."

Irsh jogged alongside. "Did he say dragon?"

Partner screamed one last time in his mind. The chains shattered, freeing him, but he was too late. The great wyrm was just above them, swooping in hard, mouth agape, feet tucked back. Partner saw the chest swell. "Dragon!"

Heads turned. Gasps.

And then the dragon breathed and a cloud of icy death engulfed them.

Partner staggered back to consciousness across a field of sharp lava crystals in his mind, bleeding and forlorn, limbs bound and rigid. He forced open his eyes.

A shadow raced across the ground in front of him, dragon shaped. Troglodytes loped the last hundred yards. Irsh lay a few yards away, eyes closed and unconscious, but apparently still breathing. Doyle appeared a few feet beyond.

Cold invaded his consciousness as he woke up and felt the stun ebb away. A great weight pressed him to the ground. Partner turned his head.

Sachesu had apparently sheltered him from the dragon's breath at the last moment. Partner was cradled against the ogre's chest, underneath him, safe. Partner reached out a hand and found several inches of ice forming a solid shield across the ogre's back.

Partner looked again at the ground and saw a field of ice in the space between he and Irsh.

The great ogre philosopher had protected him from the blast when it came.

Partner reached out and closed the ogre's eyes, once bright green, now faded in death.

Slowly, awkwardly, Partner pulled himself from under the tremendous weight of his friend and stood, careful on the sheet of new ice.

He looked down and saw Doyle blink, but saw no mind behind the eyes.

So, he was alone, facing his worst enemies, his greatest nightmare.

The great blue wyrm circled one last time and them glided in to land, as graceful as a raptor coming to roost. Two great, horn-protected eyes focused on him with keen interest.

Partner-the-dragon-worshipper fell to his knees in awe and fervor, taking the body with him. Partner-the-scholar gibbered in terror. Partner-the-adventurer glanced down at his fallen friends and whimpered.

The wyrm spoke in the vast hollow emptiness, a surprisingly rich tenor for such a deep chest. "Wuaox, bring the Isaurian thief when you kill the others. I want to know what secrets they learned."

Partner watched a troglodyte in a complicated uniform salute, sword in hand more as a swagger stick than a threat. Here was the least of the lizardkind, confronted by one of his gods. What threat could such a little creature present?

Partner-the-scholar absently cataloged the approaching troops. Troglodytes all, in good order. No wyverns were present. The great god sat on a rise and surveyed his kingdom, as was his right.

The captain, Wuaox, walked closer, sneered "We're not going to have any trouble with you, are we, thief?"

Partner-the-dragon-worshipper quietly whispered. "No, master."

Master. Master?

Partner-the-dragon-worshipper happily submitted. Partner-the-scholar itemized his sins. Partner-the-adventurer looked forward to a rough and painful death in failure.

Master?

And then a new voice entered his mind. Partner had forgotten the voice, suppressed in the grand adventure of becoming something so much greater than the gods had intended. Youngest Brother looked down at his fallen friend and contemplated a world that would never know an ogre philosopher.

In his mind, Youngest Brother screamed pure rage.

Almost faster than the eye could follow, a hand slipped under his cape and drew forth the fire lance. He had never unloaded it after the last lesson.

Perhaps, he had known it would be thus.

Youngest Brother flipped the artifact to his shoulder as his thumb found the safety and flipped it off for the first time in several millennia.

Two sturdy fingers caressed the trigger as he crossed a dragon's surprised face and a songbird suddenly awoke in his ear.

Youngest Brother screamed, aloud this time, as he stroked the trigger from rest to death.

A lightning bolt erupted from his hands, connecting his life with the great wyrm who would be his god. The intense blue light was almost too much to live through. He wanted to cease, rather than live with the shame of having watched his friend die.

Downrange, the lightning bolt liberated all of its terrible energy on the form of a great blue dragon known as Marasem.

The god fell to the ground in pieces.

A troglodyte spoke. "What?"

In his mind, Youngest Brother heard Eldest Brother scream in agony as their village burned. He turned the fire lance on the lizardman captain and pulled the trigger a second time. The troglodyte simply exploded, like a star brought to earth.

Youngest Brother took a stride forward towards the assembled troops, suddenly cowering in astonished fear.

His rage had slain a god.

He became Death itself and howled at them.

"Run!"

Like spooked antelope, they scattered, tripping over each other and trampling the fallen underfoot.

In moments, Partner-the-dragon-slayer held the field, alone.

Youngest Brother cried.

Silence.

Behind him, a voice stirred. Doyle's mind had finally returned. "Partner?"

Partner turned and walked to where the wizard sat.

Doyle rubbed his eyes and flexed his hands to restore circulation. "What happened?"

Partner saw Irsh begin to stir as well. He walked over and helped lift her to a seated position. He pulled her warm tea flask from her backpack and opened it, watched her greedily suck down the heat like a newborn kit.

Partner looked one last time before he turned back to the human wizard. "Sachesu is dead."

Doyle's mind finally registered the giant blue shape piled nearby. "What is that?"

Youngest Brother sighed. "And I have slain a god."

NINE

THE LAST WALTZ

PARTNER PULLED the trigger on the fire lance, watched the mountainside hump up suddenly under the caress of blue lightning and then collapse over the cave where they had lain Sachesu's body. Moments later, a very polite, almost diffident, avalanche subsided, burying the ogre under half a mountain.

Partner chanted the ritual under his breath as he opened the fire lance and removed the spent *ammunition magazine* reverently. It was still warm to the touch as he wrapped it in a cloth and placed it in his satchel next to the great icon, the *nav beacon*, that thing that had made the quest possible. That *ammunition magazine* would form part of the legend he would take with him when he told the tales of the great ogre philosopher who had been his friend.

He felt Irsh put a warm, comforting hand on his shoulder as he sighed. He glanced up, saw the pained smile on her face. He nodded and placed his hand over hers. Truly, friends he could have never imagined when it all began.

They turned as Doyle's voice broke the silence. "Affirmative, Stig. I see your landing glare. Put her down on the flat below us where I left the signal. We'll come down when it cools."

Partner understood every word spoken by the wizard. He had no idea what the man had just said. Instead, he turned to the east and watched a star detach itself from the morning sun, accompanied by a pulsing rumble louder and steadier than the landslide had been.

Over the rising thunder, Partner called out. "Friend Doyle, what is that?"

The wizard turned and fixed him with a deadly serious look. "That is my ship. That is *Ngoma Mwisho. The Last Waltz.*

Irsh's voice broke midway through her words. "But it's flying."

The human nodded.

Partner stepped closer as the din escalated. "Are you a god?"

The wizard shook his head. "No, Partner. I am merely a wizard. Come. There are some people I want you to meet."

PARTNER MARVELED at the great ship as it rested on the rock. Up close, it looked like a sleek, metallic beast of prey, somewhere between gray and silver in color. Doyle had called it a hammerhead shark, but Partner had never seen such a creature, so he could only guess at the comparison. He could tell that it was huge, hundreds of paces long. And that it had flown here and landed on fire. The rocks had only now cooled enough to be uncomfortable instead of lethal.

From the bow end of the shark, where Doyle had said a hammerhead would have an eye, a doorway irised open. So, eye-like. Human eyes.

A ramp slid out like a great metal tongue.

At the top, movement.

A female emerged, began to walk down the ramp. Her clothing left no doubt as to her gender, but Partner had never seen anything like the materials from which it was made. But it was the woman herself that drew his eye, and then his mind.

Like Doyle she had skin that same dark, creamy brown, and the same deep brown hair in tight curls, but cut so close on the sides he could see her skin. In her hands, she carried some strange artifact made of the magical *polymer*. From her manner, it was a weapon. She did not, quite, point it at him.

The wizard strode forward. He said something in a language Partner had never encountered before, filled with rich vowels. The woman looked closely at the wizard, and then slid the weapon into a belt pouch that hung to her thigh.

They exchanged a hug that was less than lovers and more than companions. Doyle kissed her on a cheek. He smiled and turned to face them, one hand lightly around her back, hip to hip on the side without the weapon.

Doyle gestured as he spoke. "Piper, these are my companions, Irsh and Partner."

Partner watched her mannerisms closely, learning a whole new human body language as she smiled and spoke. "*Ni vizuri kukutana na wewe.*"

Doyle translated with warmth. "She said she is pleased to meet you. Irsh, Partner, this is my niece, Piper Iwakuma-Holmström."

Irsh was silent, still shocked by the turn of events. Partner spoke up in her stead. "And we are very pleased to meet you, Friend Piper."

Piper blinked at him in surprise, and then smiled warmly. With her free hand, she pointed back over her left, disbelief evident in her tones. "*Ni kwamba joka?*"

Doyle laughed affectionately. "Indeed it is. My little friend here, Partner, killed a god."

———

THE COLLECTED GROUP sat around a fire built up of brush as the sun set, and consumed the most interesting meal Partner could have ever imagined, steaks carved from the ribs of a fallen god.

In addition to Piper, Partner had met the other two members of Doyle's crew, a towering blond human named Bjorn who was Piper's mate, and a second cousin, Stig Tjäder, who was an average-sized human with hair almost the same blood red shade as Irsh's, and a booming laugh. He sat close to Irsh and engaged in preliminary mating rituals, possibly with some success, although human interactions were still a new language for Partner.

Partner considered his friends as he chewed. The meat was tender and wonderful in his mouth, for all it left behind the taste of ashes. He missed Sachesu. He missed his friend.

Partner interrupted Doyle's stream of translation between players to ask a simple question. "Doyle, if you had this ship, this power, why all the secrecy? You could have taken anything you wanted from the troglodytes."

The murmurs died down. Doyle took a drink from a glass bottle that smelled of fermented fruit juice and settled himself. "Because it would never have helped your world."

Partner cocked his head to the side as he had learned from his friends.

Doyle grinned wryly at him. "If I did that, it would be just another war among the gods. But you, my friend, you have done something that nobody has ever done. You have slain a dragon, a god, if you will. The whole world will tremble."

He paused to repeat the words for his kin-group. They nodded and murmured.

Doyle took another sip. "And you will have tokens of that feat. And stories and witnesses. But it is necessary to move very fast right now, to exploit the situation."

He translated again, and then paused to listen to a question from Piper. "Ndiyo, Piper. Yes."

Doyle's arms expanded to encompass the group, and the whole world. "Another dragon will come, and take charge, but not before we can sneak in the back way with a few *hoversleds*, and steal all the dragon's treasure. And bring with us enough arcane *firepower* to destroy any troglodytes that wish to gainsay us."

Partner nodded. "And what will you do with the treasure, Doyle?"

The wizard paused. Partner had become adept at reading his face. Several answers were considered and discarded. "Partner, all the worlds of the Confederation fell into barbarism when the Cataclysm came. Many of them simply died. A few, like Ballard, my home, survived, but even today we cannot reproduce the artifacts of the ancients, the *technology*. That treasure will make me rich beyond any measure on this world, but it will also help all of humanity recover some of what was lost."

The wizard paused to let that sink in.

He finished his bottle and carefully opened a second one, identical. "And I promised a great reward. Irsh, I can give you wealth to make your wildest dreams come true. What do you desire?"

Partner watched the woman weigh her options. She smiled hesitantly at Stig. He returned it, just as hesitantly. She looked around the group slowly, and then glanced at the shattered hillside in the distance. "I think I would like to see what is beyond the sky."

Partner watched the wizard and his niece negotiate with eyebrow movements and nods and shakes. The outcome seemed good. "That is within my power to grant, Irshandra, daughter of Ayya. I will work you like a beast of the field, and Bjorn will teach you how to be a spacer. But the things you will see."

Doyle turned to him. "And you, Partner? Half of all this is yours. Do you wish to see the stars?"

Youngest Brother considered the crew of the strange ship, of *The Last Waltz*. He watched Irsh tentatively hold hands with Stig. He looked up at the tomb of his friend. He turned his eyes toward the wizard Doyle. The stranger who came from beyond the sky. He nodded and smiled sadly.

"It is necessary that I remain in this place, Doyle. I have a story to tell, about a great ogre philosopher, and world that needs to hear it…"

ABOUT THE AUTHOR

Blaze Ward writes science fiction in the Alexandria Station universe (Jessica Keller, The Science Officer, The Story Road, etc.) as well as several other science fiction universes, such as Star Dragon, the Collective, and more. He also writes odd bits of high fantasy with swords and orcs. In addition, he is the Editor and Publisher of *Boundary Shock Quarterly Magazine.* You can find out more at his website www.blazeward.com, as well as Facebook, Goodreads, and other places.

Blaze's works are available as ebooks, paper, and audio, and can be found at a variety of online vendors (Kobo, Amazon, and others). His newsletter comes out quarterly, and you can also follow his blog on his website. He really enjoys interacting with fans, and looks forward to any and all questions—even ones about his books!

Never miss a release!
If you'd like to be notified of new releases, sign up for my newsletter.

I will never spam you or use your email for nefarious purposes. You can also unsubscribe at any time.

http://www.blazeward.com/newsletter/

Connect with Blaze!

Web: www.blazeward.com
Boundary Shock Quarterly (BSQ):
https://www.boundaryshockquarterly.com/

facebook.com/KRPBlaze

goodreads.com/Blaze_Ward

ABOUT KNOTTED ROAD PRESS

Knotted Road Press fiction specializes in dynamic writing set in mysterious, exotic locations.

Knotted Road Press non-fiction publishes autobiographies, business books, cookbooks, and how-to books with unique voices.

Knotted Road Press creates DRM-free ebooks as well as high-quality print books for readers around the world.

With authors in a variety of genres including literary, poetry, mystery, fantasy, and science fiction, Knotted Road Press has something for everyone.

Knotted Road Press
www.KnottedRoadPress.com

www.ingramcontent.com/pod-product-compliance
Lightning Source LLC
Chambersburg PA
CBHW070913100726
47907CB00008B/2309